Dear Parents and Educators,

Welcome to Penguin Young Readers! As parents and educators, you know that each child develops at his or her own pace—in terms of speech, critical thinking, and, of course, reading. Penguin Young Readers recognizes this fact. As a result, each Penguin Young Readers book is assigned a traditional easy-to-read level (1–4) as well as a Guided Reading Level (A–P). Both of these systems will help you choose the right book for your child. Please refer to the back of each book for specific leveling information. Penguin Young Readers features esteemed authors and illustrators, stories about favorite characters, fascinating nonfiction, and more!

A Is for Amber: Orange You Glad It's Halloween, Amber Brown?	LEVEL **3**
	GUIDED READING LEVEL **K**

This book is perfect for a **Transitional Reader** who:
- can read multisyllable and compound words;
- can read words with prefixes and suffixes;
- is able to identify story elements (beginning, middle, end, plot, setting, characters, problem, solution); and
- can understand different points of view.

Here are some **activities** you can do during and after reading this book:
- Creative Writing: In this story, Amber Brown and her best friend, Justin, bring pumpkins dressed as their favorite book characters to school. Pretend you go to school with Amber and Justin and were given the same assignment. How would you decorate your pumpkin?
- Compound Words: A compound word is made when two words are joined together to form a new word. First look for the following compound words in the story: *everyone, cupcake, underpants, inside,* and *worktable.* Then, on a separate sheet of paper, write down the definition for each compound word. Next, break each word into two separate words and write down the meaning for each word.

Remember, sharing the love of reading with a child is the best gift you can give!

—Bonnie Bader, EdM
   Penguin Young Readers program

*Penguin Young Readers are leveled by independent reviewers applying the standards developed by Irene Fountas and Gay Su Pinnell in *Matching Books to Readers: Using Leveled Books in Guided Reading,* Heinemann, 1999.

To Susan Kochan —PD

PENGUIN YOUNG READERS
Published by the Penguin Group
Penguin Group (USA) LLC, 375 Hudson Street, New York, New York 10014, USA

USA | Canada | UK | Ireland | Australia | New Zealand | India | South Africa | China

penguin.com
A Penguin Random House Company

Text copyright © 2005 by Paula Danziger. Illustrations copyright © 2005 by Tony Ross. All rights reserved.
First published in 2005 by G.P. Putnam's Sons, and in 2007 by Puffin Books, imprints of Penguin Group
(USA) LLC. Published in 2014 by Penguin Young Readers, an imprint of Penguin Group (USA) LLC,
345 Hudson Street, New York, New York 10014. Manufactured in China.

The Library of Congress has cataloged the Putnam edition under the
following Control Number: 2003026637

ISBN 978-0-14-240809-4   10 9 8 7 6 5 4 3 2 1

PENGUIN YOUNG READERS

LEVEL 3

TRANSITIONAL READER

IS FOR AMBER

Orange You Glad It's Halloween, Amber Brown?

by Paula Danziger
illustrated by Tony Ross

Penguin Young Readers
An Imprint of Penguin Group (USA) LLC

I, Amber Brown, am
ready for Pumpkin Day.
So is my best friend,
Justin Daniels.
We are each taking a
pumpkin to school.
They are dressed as our
favorite book characters.

5

My parents are in

the living room, having a talk.

Something tells me it is

not a happy talk.

They have not been

getting along lately.

I hope that they make up

before tonight.

I, Amber Brown, will be wearing

the best costume ever.

It will be a sad Halloween if my
parents are not getting along.
Justin takes his pumpkin
out of the bag.
He lifts it up over his head.
The pumpkin has underpants
tacked to it.
"Captain Underpants to the rescue!"
he shouts.
The underpants cover part of
Justin's face.
There is pumpkin
juice on them.
"Are we going soon?"
Justin makes a face.

I sigh.

"I hope so."

I want to cry.

Justin puts his pumpkin
in front of his face.

"Knock, knock."

"Who's there?" I ask.

"Banana."

"Banana who?" I ask.

Justin says "Banana" again.

"Banana who?" I ask again.

That happens three more times.

I, Amber Brown, am getting
tired of bananas.

Finally Justin yells, "KNOCK, KNOCK!"

I glare.

"Who is there?
You better tell me."

Justin screams, "ORANGE!"

"ORANGE WHO?" I yell back.

"Orange you glad it's Halloween,
Amber Brown?"

I giggle and nod.

I will be very glad that
it's Halloween if my parents
don't ruin it.

That would be a bad trick,
not a good treat.

My dad rushes into the room.

"Hurry up, kids . . . or you're going
to be late."

That's not our fault, I think.

My mom comes into the kitchen.

She smiles at Justin and me.

I can't tell if everything is okay or not.

I wish I knew.

She kisses me good-bye.

Justin asks her to kiss

Captain Underpants good-bye.

She does.

Then she kisses Justin.

She doesn't kiss
my dad.

Dad picks up the cupcakes that Mom and I baked last night.

Justin, Dad, and I go out to the car.

Justin and Captain Underpants and I sit in the backseat.

My pumpkin, Lily, her purple plastic purse, and the cupcakes sit in the front with Dad.

"Amber," Justin asks, "what are you going to be for Halloween?"

"It's a surprise," I say.

"I'm not telling anyone, not even you."

Justin sticks out his tongue at me.

"Well . . . I'm not going to tell you mine either," he says.

"You're probably going as a giant booger."

I giggle.

But I don't tell him.

We get to the school and rush inside.

A pumpkin-head is standing

by the counter.

It is wearing a sign.

It's Mr. Robinson, our principal.

He signs our late passes.

We hurry to class.

Ms. Light is already teaching.

Justin and I sit down
at our desks.
Dad puts the cupcakes on
the worktable and leaves.

Ms. Light passes out papers.

I look at mine.

Five pumpkins are drawn

on the page.

We have to add eyes, noses, mouths,

and teeth to each pumpkin.

We also have to add one more thing.

I give my pumpkins

twenty freckles each.

Then Ms. Light asks,

"How many noses are there

all together?

How many eyes?

How many mouths, teeth, and

other items?"

She can't fool me.

This is supposed to be fun, but it's

really math.

I look over at Justin.

He's already finished.

I look at his paper.

He has given his pumpkins pimples.

I wonder what it would look like if a
pumpkin had its pimple squeezed.

I try counting everything again.

Hannah Burton is sitting

across from me.

She whispers, "1, 2, 11, 15, 7, 62, and 3,"

over and over, just to mix me up.

Hannah Burton is a

pumpkin pimple.

Ms. Light comes over.

She looks at my paper.

She knows I am having trouble.

She shows me how to add it up.

I put my head down on the desk.

She rumples my hair and says,

"Don't worry.

You'll be able to do this.

After all, you are one of my BRIGHT

LIGHTS."

Next, each of us stands up and tells about our pumpkin and the book it comes from.

At lunch, Justin tries to make me tell
what costume I will wear tonight.
I, Amber Brown, will NOT tell him.

After lunch, Ms. Light reads us
Space Case by Edward and
James Marshall.
Everyone laughs.
It's really funny.
A real alien from outer space
goes trick-or-treating.

I think about tonight.

What if my parents are in

a bad mood?

What if they don't do the things

we always do on Halloween?

All of a sudden, I feel sad.

What if my parents get a divorce?

Then Ms. Light says,

"Time for pumpkin jokes."

Hannah raises her hand quickly.

Ms. Light calls on her.

"How can you fix a broken pumpkin?"

Hannah asks.

Then she says, "With a pumpkin patch."

I, Amber Brown, raise my hand even higher than Hannah raised hers.

"What's black and white and orange and waddles?" I ask.

Nobody can guess.

"A penguin with a pumpkin!" I giggle.

Justin jumps up and down.
"Why did the pumpkin
cross the road?"
Before anyone can even answer,
he yells, "Because the chicken
took the day off to trick-or-treat!!!"
Everyone tells a joke.

Then it's Pumpkin Party time
with pumpkin soup, cupcakes,
cookies, bread, and pies.

School ends.

We line up to leave.

Ms. Light hands each of us

a little bag of candy pumpkins

and candy corn.

Justin offers me pieces of candy

if I tell him what my costume is.

I won't tell him.

Justin's mom picks us up.
We get into the backseat
with his brother, Danny.
I think that Danny is going to be
a dirty diaper for Halloween . . .
either that or he needs a change.

Justin and I sing pumpkin songs
all the way home.

When we get to the Daniels' house,

Justin and I use our candy corn

as fangs.

We pretend to be werewolves

to scare Danny.

Danny grabs one of the candy corns
out of Justin's mouth and eats it.
I bet that there is Justin slobber
on the corn!

The doorbell rings.

It's my mom.

We walk home.

There is a package

on our front porch steps.

I run up and take a look at it.

We've been "ghosted"!

There is a plastic pumpkin

filled with candy.

There's a piece of paper

on the present.

A ghost is drawn on the page.

There's a note on the ghost:

Your house has been visited by

the friendly Halloween ghost.

Put this picture of the ghost in your window and

then secretly deliver treats and a copy of

this note to two houses in your neighborhood.

You must do this without being seen!!!

Choose houses that do not have

ghosts in their windows!

And then you can enjoy

your treats.

Happy Halloween!

I, Amber Brown, love ghosting.

Mom and I get two treat bags ready.

She and I sneak up to the

Daniels' house.

We put the package on their steps.

We ring the doorbell and run away.

Then we sneak over to

Kelsea Allin's house.

Kelsea is a really nice

seventh-grader.

Sometimes she lets me walk her dog.

We leave the second treat there

and rush back to our house.

We fill a large bowl with
regular-size candy.
I'm glad that Mom didn't buy
"fun size" candy.
What is fun about a little
piece of candy?
Big bars are best.

Mrs. Swallow, on the next block,
gives out raisins and toothbrushes.
No one goes to her house anymore.

Dad comes home.

He is wearing light-up pumpkin

boppers on his head.

He is also carrying flowers for Mom.

"I'm sorry," Dad says.

Mom sighs, looks at me,

and then smiles at Dad.

They hug.

I, Amber Brown, am so happy.

We sit down for an early dinner.

Macaroni and cheese, carrots,

orange juice, and an orange cupcake.

Orange I glad it's Halloween dinner!

I eat quickly.

I want to hurry up and get dressed in

my new costume.

But dinner is taking a long time

because the doorbell rings a lot.

Each time we all get up

to look at the costumes

and to give out treats.

Chuckie Richetti is dressed

as a baseball card.

That is my second-favorite costume.

My first favorite will be my costume,

once I put it on.

My parents are smiling a lot.

They are smiling

at the trick-or-treaters,

at me, at each other.

I am very happy.

I am ready to get dressed

for Halloween.

Finally, dinner is finished.

Justin and his dad arrive.

Justin is dressed as a chicken.

He is wearing a big sign.

Why did the chicken cross the street ???
To get his yummy Halloween treat!!!!!!!!!!!!!!!!

I get it.

Justin is A CHICKEN JOKE!

I rush upstairs.

Mom helps me put on my costume.

She made it for me.

I go downstairs again and yell . . .

"SURPRISE!!!"

I, Amber Brown, am

"Eye, Amber Brown."

This is going to be

the most wonderful Halloween ever.